I Got the Christmas Spirit

Connie Schofield-Morrison · ILLUSTRATED BY Frank Morrison

SCHOLASTIC INC.

To the joys of my life: Nyree, Tyreek, Nia, Nasir, and Tiffani
—C. S.-M.

To my children, Nyree, Tyreek, Nia, Nasir, and Tiffani. Be good, be great!
—F. M.

ISBN 978-1-338-34202-4

Text copyright © 2018 by Consuela Morrison. Illustrations copyright © 2018 by Frank Morrison. All rights reserved. Published by Scholastic Inc., 557 Broadway, New York, NY 10012, by arrangement with Bloomsbury Children's Books. SCHOLASTIC and associated logos are trademarks and/or registered trademarks of Scholastic Inc.

12 11 10 9 8 7 6 5 4 3   18 19 20 21 22 23

Printed in the U.S.A.   40

First Scholastic printing, September 2018

Art created with oil on canvas
Typeset in Elroy and Platsch
Book design by Yelena Safronova

I woke up to the spirit of the season.

RISE AND SHINE!

I heard the spirit in the air.

DING DONG DING

I've been saving the spirit
all year long.

JINGLE   JINGLE

I sang the spirit from my heart.

I tasted the sweet
spirit crunch!

I shivered as the spirit
nipped my nose.

I swirled and twirled
around the spirit.

SWISH

SWISH

I sparkled in the
spirit of the lights.

I felt the spirit deep down in my soul.

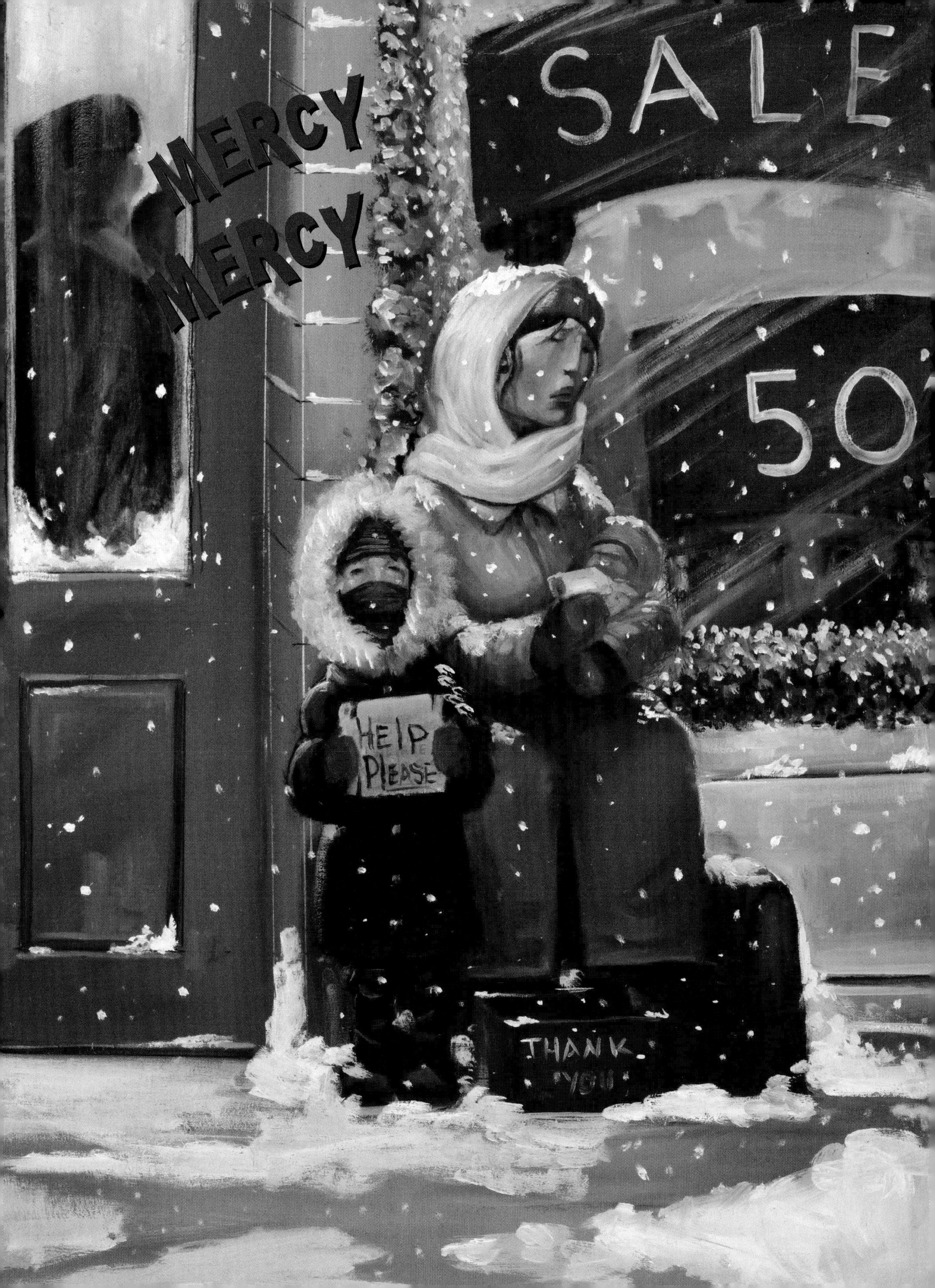
MERCY
MERCY
SALE
50
HELP
PLEASE
THANK
YOU

I chased the spirit through the store.

ZOOM

ZING

I wished for the spirit everywhere.

I spread the spirit with my smile.

The spirit is here!

The spirit is to discover something new.

Peace for all, good tidings, and cheer—
let's live the spirit every day of the year.